Super Sleuth

Super Sleuth

Twelve Solve-It-Yourself Mysteries

◼ by Jackie Vivelo ◼

Troll Associates

A TROLL BOOK, published by Troll Associates

Published by arrangement with G.P. Putnam's Sons, a division of
The Putnam Publishing Group. For information address G.P.
Putnam's Sons, a division of The Putnam Publishing Group,
200 Madison Avenue, New York, New York 10016.
First Troll Printing, 1989
Printed in the United States of America.
10 9 8 7 6 5 4 3 2
ISBN 0-8167-1547-5

To Sasha

Contents

Super Sleuth

◾1◾

The Dirty Dog

O nly one thing could ever have persuaded me to become Charles Beaghley's partner—boredom. Charlie, also known as Beagle, is the only person my age in the whole neighborhood, and nothing was happening last March. So, when he said he was starting a detective agency and wanted me for a partner, I said I'd think it over.

When he came back the next day and said he had his first case, I said, "Okay."

So now it's June. School's out, and every day I go and sit in the shed behind Beagle's house. Nothing's happening. I'm bored again. So today I went in to tell Beagle I quit.

"We'll get another job," Charlie said. "Hang around, Ellen. I'll think of something."

"Charles Beaghley, the only case we ever had was finding Mrs. Radcliffe's dog. I'm the one who did all the work, searched the neighborhood, knocked on doors. I'm the one who found the dog. And then when Mrs. Radcliffe paid us, who got the money?" I demanded.

"I split the fee with you, Ellen," the Beagle said, but he was squirming.

"Sure, but I don't like the way you split it, five dollars for me and ten for you."

"Haven't you heard of overhead?" Beagle blustered.

"Overhead! What do you have to pay for? This shed belongs to your dad, and he pays for the electricity. So what expenses do you have?"

"I bought notepads and pens!" Beagle said triumphantly. He pulled out a small notebook and handed it to me. "Stay on the job, Ellen. I've just thought of a case."

"What case? There was no case ten minutes ago."

"Uh, well, nobody's hired us for this one, but I think we can get it if we just apply. It's another missing dog."

I narrowed my eyes and glared at him with suspicion.

12

Beagle squirmed even more under my stare, and my suspicion turned to certainty.

"Charles Beaghley, if you turn dognapper, I'll never speak to you again!"

"Just once, Ellen. Twice at the most is all we'd have to do it. It would make our reputation."

"Ruin our reputations, you mean. Beagle, I think you're a crook at heart."

This seemed as good a time as any to clear out. Boy, was I ever fed up with Charlie. Beagle? Weasel, his name should be.

I walked home along the path beside Turtle Creek, kicked a few stones, and told myself I didn't care how many dogs Beagle stole and then "found" for people. He was a crook and a creep.

At home, I got out my bike and headed for Crooked Hill Road. I was halfway up the hill when I glanced back and saw Beagle, red-faced and puffing, running after me. I thought about pedaling away, but at the last second I stopped and waited for him to catch up.

It's hard to dislike somebody, even a skunk, who likes you as much as Beagle likes me.

"We've got a case!" he gasped.

"If it's another dog case, I told you to forget it."

"It's a dog case."

"Go away, Beagle. I don't want to be seen with a dognapper."

"This time you're wrong, Ellen. It is dogs, but not lost dogs and I need your help. Mrs. Thompson came over to see my mother and told her about a dog who has been digging up her garden. The problem is she doesn't know whose dog it is. So I told her we'd find out."

"Charles Beaghley, you didn't mention my name! I told you I quit."

"Sure, I did. I told Mrs. T. how you found that dog last March. She said that if we'd find the right dog for her, she would pay a reward. Those are her prize lilies he's destroying."

The next day found us combing the neighborhood for dogs. By afternoon, we had narrowed the list to four possibilities. Only those four ever roamed free in the area. The digger had to be Frisky, Bernard, Brownie or Fluffy.

By examining the flower bed and talking to Mrs. Thompson, we came up with three clues:

14

1. The digger had large paws.
2. The digger was dark-colored, but Mrs. Thompson had only gotten a glimpse of him and didn't know if he was black or brown or even how big he was.
3. He had been in the area yesterday when the last assault on the flower bed had occurred.

Combining all the information, I made up a chart.

	Dark Fur	Big Paws	Here Yesterday
FRISKY			
BERNARD			
BROWNIE			
FLUFFY			

Just one "no" in any of the three columns would be enough to eliminate a dog.

Armed with the chart, we set out to investigate our suspects.

1. Frisky turned out to be a small black-and-tan dog. He had sharp-clawed little paws that would be good at digging. We didn't

15

get a chance to talk to his owner but we did find someone who had seen him in the area yesterday.

2. Bernard was nowhere to be found, but his owner told us he was a large, brown dog who had been "around here somewhere yesterday."

3. Brownie was, of course, brown. Although she was medium-sized, she had large paws. We were lucky to get to see her since she and her owner had just come home from a three-day fishing trip.

4. Fluffy was a medium-sized ball of fluffy white fur. She had been in the neighborhood the day before. I didn't get to see her feet. They were hidden under her fur.

"Okay, Beagle," I said. "I think we've got enough."

"Which one?" Beagle asked.

"You've seen everything I have. You should know," I told him.

[Do you know? Which dog is the digger? Check your answer against Ellen's solution on the following page.]

Solution to "The Dirty Dog":

Frisky can't be the digger because he has small paws.

Brownie was away on a fishing trip. Since she wasn't here yesterday, she is innocent.

Fluffy can't be the digger because she is white, and the dog Mrs. Thompson saw was dark.

That leaves Bernard as the digger.

We reported our discovery to Mrs. Thompson, who said she would ask Bernard's owner to keep him at home. Bernard was one dog that wouldn't cause trouble anymore. I wish I could say the same for Beagle.

◼2◼

Clues in the Diary

The night we solved the case for Mrs. Thompson, Beagle and I bought a pizza and ate it in our office. We also split a box of doughnuts. I ate two. Beagle ate five.

I looked over the remaining five doughnuts: a cream-filled, a jelly-filled, two chocolate-covered, and one coconut.

"Four of those are mine, Beagle. I expect to see all five of them when I come in tomorrow morning."

"Sure, Ellen," Beagle agreed, wiping custard from his last doughnut off his chin.

In detecting there is such a thing as circumstantial evidence, the evidence of circumstances. When there's no eyewitness, circumstantial evidence is all you have to go on. The next morning circumstantial evidence told me that Beagle had kept eating doughnuts.

Doughnuts are bought by the dozen, and five had been left. When I came in the next day, there were seven doughnuts in the box. I didn't have to be there to know what had happened. Beagle had bought a second dozen.

"Charles Beaghley," I exclaimed in exasperation, "you ate ten doughnuts after I left!"

"Here, take the box," Charlie said. "I don't feel so good, and we've got a case to solve."

I have a lot to complain about. I do all the work of detecting, and Charlie eats up all the profit. But I have to admit he comes up with the cases.

"What is it?" I asked, ready to get started.

"Mrs. Wilcox, who lives in that green house by Mrs. Thompson, has an attic filled with paintings, all unsigned. They were painted by one of her great-grandmother's children. They could have been painted by her grandfather or by one of her great-aunts or great-uncles. She has a bunch of cousins, and they all want to claim the pictures. Mrs. Thompson told her we could find out who painted them."

"That's fine," I said, "but, if the pictures aren't

signed, what do we have for evidence?"

"Just part of an old diary her great-grandmother kept. She's going to show it to us this morning."

I grabbed a raspberry-cream doughnut and called out, "Let's go."

A few minutes later, we parked our bikes on Mrs. Wilcox's lawn.

She seemed really glad to see us and asked us to sit down while she told us all she knew about the problem.

"There were five children in my grandfather's family, Alvin, Rebecca, Harvey, George and Alice. I'm not going to tell you which of the three boys became my grandfather because I don't want to prejudice you.

"I'm afraid there's not a great deal I can tell you. One of the children took up painting in the 1890s and dropped it after a few years, in spite of signs of talent. The painter could have been either a man or a woman. All we know is that the paintings are in a style that recently became popular once again.

"Half my relatives suddenly remembered those old pictures and asked for them. I don't mind giving them up, but I'd like to give them to the descendant of the artist," Mrs. Wilcox concluded.

"Charles said something about a diary, Mrs. Wilcox. Would you mind if we looked at that?" I asked.

The small leather-bound book had lost its back cover and whole sections were missing. Other parts had been water-soaked and were unreadable.

For the 1890s, only three entries remained legible.

August, 1890
Alvin and the "black sheep" are going to the state university this fall.

May, 1892
Rebecca, George and my "artist" are going to spend their summer vacation traveling along the Mississippi. They will probably spend some time visiting my cousin Elaine.

June, 1892
Have terrible doubts but Alice and my "black sheep" are going to spend the summer in Europe with Uncle Russ and his family.

"Unfortunately, Mrs. Wilcox," I explained, "to identify the artist, I'm afraid we'll also have to identify the black sheep."

"Don't worry about that," she said, smiling. "My grandfather and all his brothers and sisters grew up to be fine people."

"The first diary entry," I began, "tells us that Alvin can't be the black sheep."

I drew up a grid and wrote "no" beside Alvin's name under the heading "black sheep."

	Artist	Black Sheep
ALVIN		No
REBECCA		
HARVEY		
GEORGE		
ALICE		

Mrs. Wilcox slipped from the room and returned in a few minutes with a pitcher of lemonade and a plate of doughnuts. Beagle started to groan, but it turned into a grunt as I swiftly kicked him.

"Concentrate, Beagle," I commanded. "The two people who went to Europe in the summer of 1892 didn't go traveling down the Mississippi, and the three on the Mississippi weren't going to Europe. What does that tell us?"

"Beats me," Beagle answered, absentmindedly picking up a doughnut.

[Can you solve the mystery along with Ellen? Check your answer against the solution on the following page.]

Solution to "Clues in the Diary":

Rebecca and George are not the artist. Also, neither of them is the black sheep since they traveled on the Mississippi while the black sheep went to Europe.

Alice cannot be the black sheep because she traveled with him to Europe. She cannot be the artist because the artist traveled along the Mississippi.

Only Alvin and Harvey are left. We know the artist and the black sheep cannot be the same person since one spent the summer in Europe while the other was on the Mississippi. Alvin is not the black sheep, so Alvin is the artist. Harvey is the black sheep.

"Dear old Uncle Harvey," Mrs. Wilcox said. "And dear, talented Uncle Alvin. Cousin Sylvia will be so glad."

"That means your grandfather wasn't the black sheep or the artist," I said, feeling relieved.

"Hey," Beagle contributed, "that means your grandad was George!"

Beagle had solved his first mystery.

■3■

The Old West
Challenge

I was just telling my uncle that you can solve *anything*," Beagle told me as soon as I climbed off my bike this morning.

"The trouble with bragging," I told him, "is there's always a chance somebody's going to say 'Show me.'"

"You know, you're right again," Beagle said, shaking his head in amazement. "That's just what Uncle Bob said. He told me to send you into the kitchen as soon as you got here. He has a challenge for you."

I opened my mouth to protest, and then I shut it. It's no use complaining about Beagle and the trouble he gets me into. He'll never change.

"If this is a challenge, it had better include you," I said.

"Nope, not this time," Charlie answered. "This time

24

I'm going to do something really useful."

"Like what?" I asked.

"I'm painting the name of our detective agency on the door of the shed."

I have to admit I was impressed.

"The Ellen Sloan–Charles Beaghley Detective Agency," I said, just testing it out. "No, too long," I decided. "How about the Sloan–Beaghley Detective Agency?" I suggested. "Or, you could make it Beaghley–Sloan," I added generously.

"Let it be a surprise," Beagle said. "You just go see if Uncle Bob can outsmart you."

I guess I was expecting to see an overgrown Beagle in the kitchen, so I was surprised to find a normal, intelligent-looking man.

I introduced myself to Charlie's Uncle Bob and found out that he is the author of about a dozen Western adventure novels. He said he was going to tell me a little about four characters from the Old West. Then he wanted me to figure out which one of the four was a sheriff and which one was a gunfighter.

Oh, Beagle, I thought, what have you gotten me into now?

The four names Uncle Bob gave me were Fuzzy Willis, Bill Phipps, Slow Gun Joe and Bart Lazenby.

While he talked, I jotted down notes.

A few minutes later I had the following list:

1. Fuzzy Willis and the gunfighter had been born in Wyoming. Bill Phipps had come out west from South Carolina.
2. Slow Gun Joe had warned the sheriff that the gunfighter was out to get him.
3. Bill Phipps and the sheriff had once been on a cattle drive together.
4. Both the sheriff and Bart Lazenby were expert poker players.

"Well, Ellen," Uncle Bob asked, "do you think you know which was the sheriff and which was the gunfighter?"

I looked back over my clues and quickly drew a chart:

	sheriff	gunfighter
FUZZY WILLIS		
BILL PHIPPS		
SLOW GUN JOE		
BART LAZENBY		

[Can you find the answer before looking at the next page to learn what Ellen told Uncle Bob?]

Solution to "The Old West Challenge":

Clue #1 means that neither Fuzzy Willis nor Bill Phipps is the gunfighter.

Clue #2 eliminates Slow Gun Joe as the gunfighter and as the sheriff. If you are marking your chart, you will see at this point that only one person can possibly be the gunfighter.

Clue #3 tells us that Bill Phipps is not the sheriff.

Burt Lazenby is also eliminated as the sheriff both by clue #4 and by the fact that he is the gunfighter.

Therefore, Fuzzy Willis is the sheriff.

Uncle Bob congratulated me on finding the solution to his challenge, and I hurried back outside.

I had spent half an hour talking to Uncle Bob so I didn't figure Beagle had gotten very far with the name painting. Boy, was I wrong!

Fresh black paint gleamed on the white door. I know Beagle and should have been prepared for what I saw, but I wasn't.

I wonder if you are?

The door said

THE BEAGLE DETECTIVE AGENCY
Charles Beaghley, *Owner*

"Why did you do it, Charles?" I asked. "You never detected an ant at a picnic."

"It just sounded right," he said, grinning. He was really pleased with himself.

I was mad enough to start looking around for white paint to paint over it, but Charlie distracted me with the only remark that would have worked.

He said, "Hey, while you were talking to my uncle, I found us another case!"

◼4◼

"Stop, Thief!"

W hat's up?" I asked Beagle as we hurried toward the alley behind his house.

"George Freeman's bike has been stolen. He's checking around his backyard for clues. I told him we'd be right down."

"One thing I'd like to have explained," I said, still trotting along, "is how you found a mystery while you were painting a door."

"Oh, that's easy," Beagle panted. "George came running through the yard yelling 'Thief!' I stopped him to hear what had happened, and then I told him you'd find the thief."

"Thanks, Charles," I said through clenched teeth. "What do I do if there are no clues?"

Fortunately for him we arrived at George's house just then.

"All I can tell you," George said, "is that the bike was ridden down the alley toward Warner Street and only three people have passed through the alley in the last few minutes—Carl Watkins, Stanley White and Howard Lane. They were all seen heading this way in the last half hour, and I know the bike was here before that. One of them has to be the thief, but which one?"

We followed the alley out to Warner Street where it ended. The thief had to have ridden either north or south on Warner Street.

Beagle, George and I split up and went from house to house along the street asking everybody we saw if they had seen any boys go past.

A few minutes later we met back at the alley to pool our information.

When I had written down all we had found out, I had the following notes:

1. Carl had been heard yelling at a boy with a dog. "You call that thing a dog," he had said. "It looks more like a donkey to me."

2. Mrs. Jenkins, who was watering hanging

plants on her porch, had seen the boy with the dog, but she didn't recognize him.

3. Stanley, who does odd jobs for Mrs. Jenkins, is the only one of our suspects she knows. She told us he doesn't have a dog.

4. The dog owner had been seen walking south on Warner Street, followed by Carl. The boy on a bike had been seen riding north.

"That doesn't help much," George said doubtfully.

"That's what you think," Beagle said. "Just wait till Ellen gets through sorting it out."

"Okay, we know that three boys came through the alley and three came out on Warner Street. We just have to figure out which is which," I said. "Do you know which boy was walking with a dog?" I asked George.

"Mr. Boatman was working in his garden the whole time, and he saw everybody who went past. He did say there was a Great Dane, but he didn't know which boy it belonged to."

"And he's certain nobody came out of the alley at his end?"

"He's sure." George nodded glumly.

I sketched out a chart on the notebook page.

	with dog	*with bike*
CARL		
STANLEY		
HOWARD		

[Can you sort out the information and find the thief before you read Ellen's solution on the next page?]

Solution to "Stop, Thief!":

"Let's see," I said, marking an X beside Carl's name in the column headed "with dog." "Carl didn't have the dog since we know he was teasing the guy who did.

"We also know Stanley doesn't have a dog. So it looks like the dog belongs to Howard.

"The dog owner was walking in the opposite direction from the thief, so that eliminates Howard as the thief.

"We can also put an X beside Carl's name under the bike heading since he was walking in the same direction the dog owner was.

"And that means Stanley has your bike," I concluded, showing George the chart, which now looked like this:

	with dog	with bike
CARL	X	X
STANLEY	X	O
HOWARD	O	X

"Thanks," George called, as he set off at a run for Stanley's house. "You saved the day!"

Beagle and I, left to ourselves, started back along the alley, suddenly aware that it was lunchtime.

▣5▣

Uncle Bob's
Real Mystery

I had just finished eating lunch when the phone rang. It was Beagle calling to tell me his uncle needed our help.

"Do you mean he really needs help, or is this just another test?"

"It's for real. He says he is sure you can handle it and save him some time."

A few minutes later I was back at Beagle's house, sitting at the kitchen table while I watched him finish off a coconut cream pie.

"Uncle Bob's gathering up some of his research material. He'll be down in a few minutes. Are you sure you don't want any of this pie?" The last bite of the last piece disappeared down his throat as he asked me.

Uncle Bob's arrival saved me from answering. He came in with a stack of books and papers, dumped them at the end of the table, and sat down.

"Even though the books I write are fiction," Uncle Bob explained, "I always do research before I write. Sometimes the made-up characters in my books meet historical characters. When I include some from the real Western past, I like to be accurate.

"Now, in this new book Cal Smith, my own character, is going to be involved with a real-life gang that terrorized the western part of Texas for more than two years. The problem is that very little reliable information is available. What I do have is a copy of an authentic note written in 1884. It's not much to go on, but from what I've seen you can handle it. Are you willing to give it a try, Ellen?"

"I won't make any promises. But, sure I'll try it."

"Fine," Uncle Bob said. "First, let me tell you the names of the gang members."

"Just a sec," I said, whipping open my notebook and getting set to write. "Okay, I'm ready."

"They were known as the Panhandle Gang, and their names were Tyler, Morrison, Corbett and Franklin. Like most Western bad guys and heroes too," Uncle

Bob went on, "these men had nicknames. They were known as Rustler, Kid, Chew-Tobacco Charlie and the Gunman."

I wrote the names in one column and the nicknames in another in my notebook.

"Sometimes the men are referred to by their own names and sometimes by their nicknames. For instance, I know the gang was formed by the man called the Rustler, but I don't known which one he is. And that's where you come in, Ellen. I want you to help me match names and nicknames. This is the kind of thing that really slows me down. You'll be making a big contribution to my next book if you can work this out."

Uncle Bob pushed a slip of paper across the table to me. Beagle abandoned his empty plate to move into the seat next to me and read along with me.

CORBETT,
    We want you to join up with us. If yer willin, come to Willow Creek Camp on Saturday.
    Morrison and me will make sure the Gunman can be counted in.
    Don't tell the Kid I have writ to you. Franklin and the Kid won't be told yer joinin us until you show up.
                                        RUSTLER

As soon as we had read through the note, Uncle Bob said, "How about starting with Corbett and trying to match him with one of the nicknames?"

"First, I'm going to jot down some information from this letter," I said.

A couple of minutes later I was looking over the following list in my notebook:

1. Corbett received a message from the Rustler asking him to join forces with a gang that was being formed.
2. According to the message, Morrison and the Rustler were going to persuade the Gunman to join the gang.
3. Corbett was told not to mention the note to the Kid.
4. Franklin and the Kid were not to be told Corbett was going to join the gang.

Below the list I made the following chart:

	Rustler	Gunman	Kid	Chew-Tobacco Charlie
CORBETT				

"This one's easy," I told Uncle Bob.

[Before you look ahead at the solution on the next page, see if you can find the answer for yourself. Got it? Okay, read on.]

As soon as I had answered, Uncle Bob said, "I guess that was kind of obvious, but it looked impossible before we singled him out. How about taking Morrison next? Can you match him with a nickname?"

So I sketched out another chart.

	Rustler	Gunman	Kid
MORRISON			

"Note #2 answers this one," I said.

"Great," Uncle Bob said. "Now tell me Franklin's nickname."

"It gets easier," I said, "as we eliminate."

This time my chart only had two choices.

	Rustler	Gunman
FRANKLIN		

Notes #1 and 4 solved this one.

"And, of course, that tells us who Tyler was," Uncle Bob said. "This is a great help. If you two will excuse me, I'll get started on my book."

38

Solution to "Uncle Bob's Real Mystery":

Corbett's identity: The Rustler wrote the note to Corbett. The Kid and the Gunman are both mentioned in the note. So Corbett is Chew-Tobacco Charlie.

Morrison's identity: Since Morrison can't be either the Rustler or the Gunman, according to clue #2, he is the Kid.

Franklin's identity: Since Franklin is not going to be told about the note, he cannot be the Rustler. Therefore, he is the Gunman.

Tyler's identity: The only nickname that remains is "the Rustler." So Tyler is the Rustler and the leader of the gang, as well as the author of the note.

I went out the door to go home and Beagle went along with me.

"Now can we change the name to 'The Ellen Sloan Detective Agency'?" I asked just as we reached Turtle Creek.

Beagle slowed down and came to a halt. "You know, Ellen," he said, "you couldn't have done it without me."

"What do you mean, Charles Beaghley?" I asked, as he started back toward his own house.

"*I* gave you the notebook," Charlie called back and kept on walking home.

∎6∎

Sloan Alone

When I left Beagle yesterday, I made up my mind I was through. He is without any doubt the most selfish person I have ever known. This time I didn't bother telling him I had quit.

The phone started ringing as I walked out the door this morning.

"Ignore it," I said to myself. "Just keep walking."

Actually I didn't walk. I ran. If I didn't answer the phone, my mother would. I didn't want to be close enough for her to call me back.

For a while I just wandered around, wishing I had had the sense to sign up for summer camp. It's not just that there are no other twelve-year-olds. I mean there is *nobody* around here to hang out with except, of course, Beagle. And, since yesterday, he no longer counts.

Maybe I could set up as a detective on my own. I thought about it for a while and wondered how I would find cases. I have to give Beagle credit for that. He does keep tripping over problems.

Around eleven o'clock, I decided to write out a notice and put it up on the bulletin board of the One-Stop Food Shop.

I went home to get an index card. As soon as I walked through the door, Mom told me Beagle wanted me to call him.

"Uh, thanks," I said. "I'm in kind of a hurry, so I'll talk to him later."

About two years later would suit me. I got the card and wrote:

ELLEN SLOAN
Pets Found—Problems Solved

I decided my printing looked pretty good, so I added my address and phone number. Then I rode to the One-Stop. Mr. Brandon, the manager, was there at the front when I went in. He doesn't know me, but I know him, because his name and picture are on the wall under the clock. He smiled and nodded at me when he saw I had a notice for the bulletin board.

Then he read the card. I could tell he wasn't interested but was just looking at it to be polite. When he had read it, he straightened up and his expression changed completely.

Just for a minute I thought there must be some sort of rule against that kind of notice.

"Are *you* Ellen Sloan?" Mr. Brandon asked.

"Yes, sir. Is there something wrong with my notice?"

He ignored my question.

"My wife mentioned you. She had heard how you solved a problem for a friend of hers. Something to do with some old paintings. Are you that Ellen Sloan? Of course, you must be. There couldn't be two girl detectives named Ellen Sloan."

I just smiled. He seemed to be doing fine with the conversation all by himself.

"I wonder if you could step into my office a minute. I have a problem you might be able to help with."

"Sure," I said.

He had to stop twice to speak to people, and there was a phone call for him when we got to his office. Altogether, ten minutes passed before he told me why he wanted to talk to me.

"Maybe I'm crazy, telling this to a kid. But I don't want to call the police."

"What's the problem, Mr. Brandon? If I can't help, I'll tell you."

"To put it bluntly, one of my stockboys is a thief. He's not stealing money. We take plenty of precautions with the cash. Anybody fiddles with that and we know who immediately.

"No, the trouble is that cases of food are being stolen. The food is being removed from the premises during working hours by one of my employees. So far I've narrowed it down to the boys who work the evening shift, and I've been able to eliminate the possibility that they are in this together. It's one of these four," Mr. Brandon concluded, handing me a slip of paper.

I read the list of names—John Holt, Will Campbell, Tommy Reeves, Curtis Logan. Quickly, I copied them into my notebook.

"If you would like, you can bag groceries for a few days until you come to some conclusion," Mr. Brandon suggested.

Mr. Brandon suggested the names of employees he thought I should talk to first. "I'll talk to you again at four o'clock," he told me. "I'd like to know how you're doing, and we'll decide if it's worthwhile for you to continue."

As I talked to the employees during the afternoon, I realized that several of them knew all about the food thief. But not one person was willing to accuse one of the stockboys. However, I did find out some things:

1. Three of the boys come to work by car. One of them rides a motorcycle.
2. Will and the motorcyclist have both tried to persuade the thief to turn himself in.
3. John and Tommy both ride to work together in John's car.
4. Tommy and the thief have been friends since high school.

It didn't seem like much, but I had an idea that it would tell me which boy was the thief.

My chart looked like this:

	Motorcylist	Thief
JOHN		
WILL		
TOMMY		
CURTIS		

At four o'clock, Mr. Brandon called me back into his office.

"Have you found the thief?" he asked, smiling to show he didn't really expect results so soon.

"Yes, sir," I answered.

[Do you know who the thief is?]

Solution to "Sloan Alone":

We know from clue #2 that Will is not the motorcyclist. Neither is John or Tommy, as we see in clue #3. That means that Curtis is the motorcyclist. We know from clue #2 that the motorcyclist is not the thief and neither is Will. Clue #4 reveals that Tommy is not the thief. So, John is the one who has been stealing food.

Riding home on my bike that evening, I thought about Beagle and wondered how it felt to have a detective agency and no detective.

◼ 7 ◼

The Case of
the Missing Book

This is just my second day without Beagle, and I walked right into another problem to solve. At first it looked like nothing was going to happen all day, but late this afternoon I biked over to the library and found a case waiting for me.

Mrs. Reneker was alone at the checkout desk as I went in, and was she frantic! I thought wringing your hands in panic was something people only did in books, but she was taking turns twisting her hands together and pressing one hand to each cheek.

When I asked her what was wrong, the story came spilling out. It seems that she had brought a book from the rare books collection out to the front desk intending to return it as soon as she had checked an entry in the card file.

"It's a priceless book, one we never, ever allow out of the library," she said. "And now it's gone. It isn't just that I'll lose my job. I really do care about these books."

"A book thief!" I cried. "I never thought I'd have a chance to catch a book thief."

"No, no, you don't understand. The book wasn't stolen. It was taken by mistake. A boy came to the checkout desk with several books and laid them on the counter. Then, after I had stamped them, he slid the whole stack into a satchel, a canvas book bag. I'm sure he took that priceless old volume with him, but it was a mistake."

"Just stay calm. We'll soon figure out who he was. Don't you have a list of who checked out what?"

"Well, yes, but it's not that simple. Several people were checking out books at that time, and I don't remember who he was or which books were his."

It took several more minutes of conversation before we began to make any progress. After eliminating all the adults and girls who had been through the checkout in the past few minutes, we came up with a list of four boys who had checked out books in the last half hour.

I wrote down Sam Michaels, Jerry Stoner, Lenny Thomas and Ray Dover.

"It must be one of these," Mrs. Reneker said hopefully.

By prodding her memory and by asking questions of the other people in the library. I came up with the following information:

1. The boy with the book bag came into the library at the same time as Ray Dover and another boy who was wearing a red shirt.
2. Lenny Thomas was overheard talking to the boy in the red shirt about pirate stories.
3. Both the boy in the red shirt and the boy with the book bag were talking to Jerry Stoner about the swim meet.

Below my list of clues I sketched out a chart and went to work sorting out the suspects.

	book bag	red shirt
SAM MICHAELS		
JERRY STONER		
LENNY THOMAS		
RAY DOVER		

I knew for sure that the boy with the red shirt was not the boy with the book bag. And the boy with the book bag was the boy with the missing book. I considered my clues for a few minutes just to be certain, and then I told Mrs. Reneker the good news.

[Do you know the name of the boy with the book bag? Check your answer against Ellen's on the next page. Hint: You will need to find and eliminate the boy with the red shirt in order to identify the boy with the book bag.]

Solution to "Case of the Missing Book":

Who is the boy in the red shirt? Who is the boy with the book bag? Clue #1 tells us that Ray Dover was not wearing a red shirt or carrying a book bag. From clue #2, we learn that Lenny Thomas was not the boy in the red shirt. Jerry Stoner, as we see in clue #3, is neither the boy with the book bag or the boy in the red shirt.

At this point, it is clear that Sam Michaels must be the boy in the red shirt. Since we know that the boy in the red shirt is not the boy with the book bag, Sam Michaels is now eliminated as the possible owner of the book bag. Therefore, the boy with the book bag must be Lenny Thomas.

I offered to track Lenny Thomas down and return the book before the library closed. Mrs. Reneker gratefully accepted my offer.

For the rest of the afternoon I felt like a real private eye, a gumshoe, a 'tec. Here I was on the trail of a suspect. When I didn't find him at home, I learned that he had been seen heading south on Winslow Lane.

After a lot of tracking, I finally located Lenny at the ball park across from the apartment building where he lives. There he was, almost in sight of the very first place I had looked.

"Yeah, I noticed that weird ol' book. In fact, I was on my way back to the library when Shorty Mullins asked me to pitch."

The book was tucked under a park bench. Lenny retrieved it for me and thanked me for saving him a trip back to the library.

"Well," I thought, "I wasn't much of a hero this time. The book would have been returned in an hour or so anyway."

But Mrs. Reneker didn't see it that way.

She spent so much time thanking me that I felt lucky to get away. Outside the library I climbed on my bicycle and started home.

◾8◾

Pizza Puzzle

I had reached the corner of the street where I live when I saw Danny Dinello. He delivers pizza for his dad and works in the pizza parlor. His little blue car with the picture of the pizza on the door was pulled off onto the grass. The door was open on the driver's side of the car, and Danny was sitting there looking confused.

"Hi, Danny," I called, even though I didn't think he knew who I was, although I have bought about a hundred pizzas from him. Just on impulse I added, "Is something wrong?"

"Yeah, there is," Danny answered. "Hey, aren't you Ellen Sloan?"

"Yes, I am. Can I help you?"

"Maybe you could at that. I have these three pizzas to deliver, and I have these three names and addresses. But the delivery slips got shuffled, and I don't know which order goes to which family."

"Maybe I can help. I'll give it a try," I offered.

I asked Danny for the names of the people he was supposed to deliver to. He read them to me, and I copied them down in my notebook: Mr. Burks, Mrs. Adler, and Mr. Harris.

"Now then, tell me everything you can remember about the orders," I suggested.

I didn't know if we were going to learn anything helpful, but Danny had certainly cheered up, now that we were taking some definite action.

"I took two of the orders myself, and Dad took the other call. If I could just remember the orders I took, it would help. But it's no use. I've thought about it so much that I've confused myself."

"Just tell me what you can remember," I urged.

"The orders were for a large pepperoni, two medium plain pizzas, and a large anchovy. But how am I going to match them up with the people who ordered them?

"I know I took the call from Mr. Burks, but I can't

remember what he ordered, so that's no help."

"Well, it's something," I said doubtfully, "but you must remember something else."

"Dad must have taken the order for the two plain pizzas." Danny was beginning to look dejected again.

"You said you took two calls," I reminded him. "Can't you remember anything about the other order."

"Yes," Danny said. "I spoke to a woman."

"But you don't know what she ordered?"

"No, except that I'm sure it wasn't the anchovies."

"That should do it," I said, grinning at Danny. "Just give me a minute."

I drew a chart below the notes I had taken. The page in my notebook now said:

1. Danny took the order from Mr. Burks.
2. Danny's dad took an order for two plain pizzas.
3. Danny spoke to the only woman who called and she did not order anchovies.

	Plain	Pepperoni	Anchovy
MR. HARRIS			
MRS. ADLER			
MR. BURKS			

I filled in the chart with X's and O's, so that in a few seconds it looked like a game of tic-tac-toe. And Danny was the winner. I had matched up a pizza order with each name.

[Can you sort out the orders before you turn the page and read Ellen's solution?]

Solution to "Pizza Puzzle":

"How did you do that?" Danny asked.

"You were sure Mrs. Adler didn't order the anchovy. And, since you took her call but didn't take the call for the plain pizzas, she had to have ordered the pepperoni.

"That meant Mr. Burks couldn't have ordered the pepperoni. You did take his order but not the order for plain pizzas, so Mr. Burks ordered the anchovy.

"And that leaves the plain pizzas as the Harris order."

"Thanks a million!" Danny said. "I have to get these delivered before they get any colder."

"You're welcome, but maybe now you can solve a mystery for me. There's an extra pizza here. Who does it belong to?"

"Oh, that's an extra large pizza with everything. There's no way I could forget who ordered that one. That one's for that kid they call the Beagle. His name's Charlie or something. Hey, he's the one I've seen you with in the pizza parlor. Does he live near here?"

"The third house over there on the left."

"Great! Would you do me one more favor? Deliver his pizza. Tell him this one's free if he'll share it with you. And, thanks again."

Danny grinned and dumped the pizza into the basket of my bike. I opened my mouth to say "No, absolutely not." But, before I could speak, he drove away, leaving me and the pizza on the roadside.

◼9◼

Super Sleuth

I had believed nothing Beagle did would ever surprise me again. But I guess I didn't have him completely figured out yet.

The door to the shed was standing open, and I could see Beagle sitting at his desk when I got to his house with the pizza. "The Beagle Detective Agency . . . Charles Beaghley, Owner" was still printed on the door.

When Beagle saw me, he jumped up and came rushing around the desk. I thought for a second he was going to tackle me.

"Ellen!" he cried. "I've been looking everywhere for you."

"I brought your pizza," I said in a frosty voice.

60

And here's where the surprise came.

"Never mind the pizza. I need your help." He put the box on the desk and grabbed my arm. It was the first time I ever saw him distracted from food. "Mrs. Steele wants us to solve a problem for her."

"Solve it yourself," I said. This time there was ice in my voice.

Beagle just looked puzzled. "You know *I* can't solve mysteries," he said.

"It's your detective agency, so go and detect something."

Beagle shook his head in bewilderment. "I don't know what you're upset about. You're the detective," he said. "I'm just your business partner."

"And that means," I said, "that you get the desk, the rewards, and your name on the door. Even that pizza ought to be mine."

"Oh, well, here. Take the pizza." He picked up the box, shoved it back into my arms. "But please, even if you don't care about our agency anymore, just help Mrs. Steele. I told her I'd find you yesterday, and she has been calling every hour. That's why I came out here so I wouldn't have to keep telling her I hadn't found you. You see what a lousy detective I would be.

I can't even find a lost detective."

"Okay," I agreed, sighing and putting the pizza back on his desk. "I'll go talk to Mrs. Steele, but this is it. I don't want to be your partner, Beagle Beaghley."

"All right," said Beagle—a meek, subdued Beagle.

We started out the door and Beagle said, "Just a minute."

He turned back, opened the pizza box, and took out a slice.

"Here," he growled. "You look hungry and I already ate. You can't detect on an empty stomach."

At the Steeles' house, I found out that Mrs. Steele's problem wasn't serious and didn't involve anything criminal, but it was really important to her.

"Charles tells me you can solve any problem," she said.

"I'm not sure about that," I said.

Mrs. Steele had just celebrated her birthday and displayed on her dining-room table were four beautiful gifts: a silver tray, an ice-cream maker, a necklace-and-earrings set and a clay moisture cooker.

"These are gifts from my grown-up daughters. I love all the gifts and I'm very grateful. But, oh, I'm so embarrassed! You see, I don't know which gift is from which daughter. Please help me," she said.

This wasn't going to be easy. I even had a feeling that, while this might not be my most important case, it just might be my toughest case.

Little by little Mrs. Steele told me about her birthday.

"Melissa was the first to arrive. Carole and Diane arrived together a few minutes later. And Sharon was half an hour late. I remember Diane and Melissa both exclaimed in delight at the ice-cream maker. That was the first gift I opened.

"Oh, and Melissa said she was glad she hadn't bought a moisture cooker because that had been her first idea.

"The necklace and earrings were wrapped in blue paper, tied with silver lace ribbon. I heard Melissa say, 'Where on earth did you find that beautiful ribbon?' But I was so busy opening the present I don't remember who answered her or even what else was said.

"I had already opened both the ice-cream maker and the necklace and earrings before Sharon arrived. And that's really all I can tell you," she concluded.

It wasn't much to go on, and I was tired and hungry,

but I was willing to give it a try. I drew a chart in my notebook and then sat studying the page which now looked like this:

1. Melissa, Carole and Diane were all at the party before Sharon, who arrived half an hour late.
2. Diane and Melissa were pleased and surprised by the first gift that was opened, which was the ice-cream maker.
3. Melissa had considered buying a moisture cooker but didn't.
4. Melissa asked where the wrapping paper on the necklace-and-earrings set had been bought.
5. Sharon did not arrive with her gift until after the ice-cream maker and the necklace and earrings had been opened.

	ice-cream maker	silver tray	cooker	necklace and earrings
MELISSA				
CAROLE				
DIANE				
SHARON				

[Can you figure out who brought which gift? Ellen is right in thinking this is a very difficult puzzle. If you run into difficulties, try to work on one person at a time—just the way you did to solve "Uncle Bob's Real Problem." Start with Melissa. Then go to Sharon next. Try Diane next and leave Carole for last. When you have identified a gift for one person, remember to eliminate that gift for the other people.]

Solution to "Super Sleuth":

Melissa did not give the ice-cream maker (clue #2), the cooker (clue #3), or the necklace and earrings (clue #4). So, her gift is the silver tray.

Sharon did not give the ice-cream maker or the necklace and earrings (clue#5). Of course, she did not give the silver tray. So, her gift was the cooker.

The only gifts left now are the ice-cream maker and the necklace and earrings.

Diane did not give the ice-cream maker (clue #2). Therefore, Diane's gift was the necklace-and-earrings set. By process of elimination, we now know that Carole gave the ice-cream maker.

In a few minutes I said, "Okay, I've got it."

"How?" asked Beagle. "You couldn't possibly know enough."

"Sure I do. Here, you try it," I offered, sketching a blank grid for him.

Beagle stared at it, shook his head, and shoved it back. "Only a super sleuth could solve that one," he said.

I showed my completed grid to Mrs. Steele, who thanked me and agreed with Beagle that it had been a problem for a super detective.

Somehow I didn't feel quite so angry with Beagle anymore. When we left Mrs. Steele's house, I walked back to the shed behind his house with him. We sat at the desk and ate the pizza. Actually, I ate the pizza. Beagle only had one piece. He stood outside the partly opened door, watching the stars, he said. We called out to each other once in a while, but mostly I was busy finishing off the cold pizza.

When I was ready to go home, I stood up and stretched.

"Look at this," Beagle said, "and tell me what you think."

The door opened into the room, and Beagle pushed it completely open. I had a full view of the words painted on the door. The same ones as before were still there, but something had been added. Instead of watching the stars, Beagle had been putting paint squiggles on the door. Now it said

THE BEAGLE DETECTIVE AGENCY

Ellen Sloan, *Super Sleuth*   Charles Beaghley, *Owner*

◼10◼

The Circus Mystery

Beagle didn't bother with the telephone today. He just showed up at my door before I had finished breakfast. That didn't worry him at all. He sat down and started to eat.

"Don't you eat at home?" I asked, as he piled strawberry jam on toast.

"Of course," he said indignantly. "I ate, but that was hours ago. Well, one hour at least."

"Why are you here?" I asked.

"Because we have a case. What else?"

I still wasn't sure I wanted to share another case with Beagle, but I was curious to know what he had in mind.

"I really found this one by accident," he continued.

"You know the circus is here at the fairgrounds. My dad is one of the administrators. Last night when I got home the circus manager was there discussing a problem with Dad. So I listened in."

"I hope you didn't tell them I would solve it," I interrupted.

"What kind of dope do you take me for? I only told them you could solve it if I talked you into trying."

"Oh, great," I said, but Beagle ignored the lack of enthusiasm.

"We've got a chance to visit behind the scenes at the circus, and afterward we get in to watch the matinee for free."

"For free, if we solve the problem. What if we don't?" I asked.

"We can go to the matinee anyway. I already have the passes. Mr. Monahan, the manager, gave them to me. But why worry? You always solve everything. If you've finished breakfast, we can get started."

"Since you've eaten everything, I guess I have to be finished."

Beagle looked over the table in surprise. "And it's a good thing,. too. You would have been here all day."

Maybe I was stupid to go back into partnership with Beagle, but I couldn't resist the circus.

At the fairgrounds we asked for Mr. Monahan and were directed to the trailer that was his office and his living quarters.

"I haven't explained anything to Ellen yet," Beagle told him. "I thought it would be best for her to hear the whole story from you."

Mr. Monahan didn't seem bothered at all by the fact that we were a couple of kids. That was my first indication that circus people don't see the world quite the same way other people do. He asked us to sit down and then began to explain.

"The problem is one group of my clowns. They're the best I have and I just can't understand it. Anyway, this group consists of five guys who do a stunt-car routine and a water battle. Both are favorites with the audience." Mr. Monahan shook his head as though he still couldn't believe what he was about to tell us.

"I have had an anonymous tip-off from a member of the group telling me that two other members of the group are planning to sabotage a new clown act I'm introducing on this tour."

"That means they're going to find a sneaky way to

70

ruin the other guys' performance," Beagle explained.

"I know that, but how did you know?" I asked Beagle.

"I looked it up last night when I heard my dad and Mr. Monahan talking."

"I have to find out who these two people are and talk to them before they make fools of themselves and a wreck of the show," Mr. Monahan said.

"The person who tipped you off to the plot knows who the plotters are. Why didn't he tell you?" I asked.

"Oh, I have no doubt that every member of the group knows about the plot—who, where, when and what. But getting them to talk is another matter. Whatever they may know, there isn't one that would willingly get any of the others in trouble. Members of an act can fight and feud among themselves, but when it comes to dealing with the rest of the world they are loyal," Mr. Monahan explained.

"Then how am I going to get the information we need?"

"I want you to talk to them. They'll talk freely enough once you're introduced. The one thing they won't give you is names," Mr. Monahan answered. "Get all the information you can and then see what you can make of it. Beagle here says you can come up with the truth from just a few hints. Just try. That's all I ask. If you fail, I'll have to face a showdown with the whole group. That's something I want to avoid if at all possible."

Before we left his office Mr. Monahan gave us the names of the clowns who performed together in the water fight and stunt cars. I copied into my notebook—Gloober, Toffy, Doctor Slick, Cappo and Socks.

"That's the strangest list of suspects we've ever had," Beagle remarked, reading over my shoulder.

Mr. Monahan found Doctor Slick first and introduced us, asking him to make sure we met the other members of the team.

For the rest of the morning we were immersed in clown activities: We watched Cappo and Socks work through a juggling routine. We met Toffy, and I helped him repair a pop-up flower on his lapel. It wasn't always easy but eventually we had managed to talk to each of the clowns alone, always keeping in mind that two of them were the plotters.

Since I didn't want to put the guilty pair on guard, I found it hard to talk to any of them. But Beagle didn't.

I had just finished working on Toffy's flower when Beagle motioned for me to take a walk with him.

"Where did you disappear to?" I asked. "I don't know how to question these people."

"Socks is scared of the plotters, but he told the plot to one of the other clowns, who then wrote the tip-off," Beagle told me.

"Did Socks tell you who the tipster was?"

"He wouldn't say."

"Still, it is a clue," I said.

"That's not all," Beagle continued. "Cappo warned the plotters not to try anything rough. He doesn't know anything about a tipster."

"That's great, Beagle. I don't know how you do it. Have you found out anything else?"

"That's all for now, but I'll keep trying. I'll meet you later."

And with that Beagle was gone.

The next time I saw Beagle was at lunch, which we ate in a tent with all the circus people.

"I found out a little more," Beagle whispered. "I'll tell you after we eat."

While we were eating, Gloober told Beagle he should consider becoming a clown.

"You are naturally funny. See," he said, pointing to the way Beagle holds his arms when he eats. "And you wouldn't even have to make up a name."

"Beagle, the clown," Socks said. "It sounds good."

After lunch, Beagle and I walked out across a field together away from the tents to be sure no one would overhear us talking.

"I hope you found out something," I said. All that had happened to me was that one of the clowns had given me a can of exploding worms. Another had squirted me with water. Another had sprayed foam in my hair. And all of that was just in fun.

"Well, I heard a couple more things. I don't know if they'll be any help."

"Anything is better than the nothing we have now."

"Okay. Gloober, Toffy, and the tipster have been secretly working out a new routine. I also learned that the two spoilers have no idea that there is a tipster in the group. It's not much, is it?"

"I think that's pretty terrific, Beagle. If we don't have enough information, it won't be your fault. After all, I haven't found a single clue."

We sat down under some trees so I could organize the information Beagle had gathered. We now had four clues:

74

1. Socks told the plot to the tipster but was too afraid of the plotters to do anything himself.
2. Cappo had warned the plotters against doing anything rough, but he didn't know there had been a tipster.
3. Neither of the two plotters knew about the tipster.
4. Gloober, Toffy, and the tipster have been secretly working on a new routine.

"That may just tell us all we want to know, Beagle," I said. "Let me give it a try."

My graph looked like this:

	plotters	tipster
GLOOBER		
TOFFY		
DOCTOR SLICK		
CAPPO		
SOCKS		

[Can you solve the problem before you turn the page to read Ellen's solution? Remember that there will be *two* plotters and one tipster. Hint: Find the tipster first.]

Solution to "The Circus Mystery":

Socks is not the tipster, clue #1. Cappo is not the tipster, clue #2; and neither are Gloober or Toffy, clue #4. Therefore, the tipster was Doctor Slick.

Socks is not one of the plotters, clue #1. Cappo is not one of the plotters, clue#2. The tipster is not one of the plotters, clue #3; therefore, Doctor Slick is not one of the plotters.

That means that Gloober and Toffy are the two plotters.

We were able to take the news to Mr. Monahan and still get to the matinee in plenty of time to watch the show. I love the circus, but every time I saw someone sprayed with foam, squirted with water, or shocked by a buzzer, I felt like it was happening to me. The morning hadn't bothered Beagle, though. In between shouting and laughing, he had five hot dogs, three sodas, a candy apple, two boxes of popcorn and cotton candy.

▣11▣
The Big
Diamond Robbery

I f the police haven't caught the thief by now, I'm afraid they won't at all." Mrs. Lockridge was close to tears as she explained to me and Beagle that her diamonds had been stolen. "I know you haven't done anything like this before, but I have to try everything. The police have investigated. I hired a private detective from the city, and he investigated. But so far no one has found the thief or the diamonds."

"I would like to help you, Mrs. Lockridge," I said. "But, if the police and a private detective have failed, well, I don't think we will have much success either."

"Hey, wait a minute!" Beagle almost shouted. "We can't quit before we even start. We may even have an advantage over the adults. Nobody would think twice about telling us things they wouldn't say to an official investigator. Please, Ellen, let's try."

"Well . . ."

"Ellen, Charles is right," Mrs. Lockridge said. "You two may just be my last hope. Please try. That's all I ask."

"All right," I agreed. I smiled at her and tried to look more encouraging than I felt.

A few minutes later, as we walked back to the shed behind Beagle's house, I repeated my doubts. "I don't see how we can possibly help Mrs. Lockridge. We have never tried to solve a real police case before."

"Some of the problems you've solved would have been police cases. The only reason the police weren't called is because you solved the case. Theft is theft," Beagle argued.

"You sound like you're just about to say that if I can solve one, I can solve them all. And that's not true, Beagle. Everything depends on how much information we collect. And in this case I don't see how we can collect any."

"You leave that to me," Beagle said.

"What can you do?"

"Never mind. Just wait and see."

78

I went home for lunch feeling pretty discouraged. Then, early in the afternoon Beagle called to say he was at the police station and asked me to hurry on over there. Since I had a vague idea that he had gotten himself arrested for interfering in police business, I got there as fast as I could.

Far from being arrested, Beagle was settled in for a friendly visit with a police captain.

"This is Captain Holloway," Beagle said. "He has been giving me some information on the Lockridge theft."

"Have a seat, Ellen. I was just explaining to Charlie here that we would welcome your help. You see, we have narrowed the investigation to three suspects, Buzz Hughes, Louis Sherwin and Lightfingers Ted Young. We know that all of these men have engaged in criminal acts, although only one of them—Lightfingers—has ever served a prison sentence. Young is currently a member of a gang suspected of shoplifting, but so far we can't tie him to this robbery. All our work has led to dead ends."

"Was the robbery the work of just one man?" Beagle asked.

"One of these three suspects stole the diamonds,"

the captain answered, "but whoever did it is a member of a well-organized gang."

"How in the world did you manage that?" I asked as soon as Beagle and I were outside the police station.

"Easy," Beagle said. "I know Captain Holloway, because he is a friend of my dad. I also know the police occasionally share information with first-rate private investigators."

"First-rate? Do you mean us?"

"Of course. The Beagle Detective Agency has never failed."

I groaned. "Don't remind me. I think you just pushed us into our first failure."

"Ellen, you are a pessimist," Beagle said. "I have a phone call to make. I'll meet you at our office in half an hour."

When Beagle showed up at the office, he was waving a sheet of paper covered with his horrible, scrawling handwriting.

"I can't read that. Nobody could read that. What does it say?" I asked.

"This is information from the private detective Mrs. Lockridge hired. She gave me his number, and I called him. He says he was investigating the same men the police were. He thinks that what he found out is of no help, but he told me everything he learned anyway," Beagle explained. "The detective spent a lot of time on the streets, talking to crooks and to people who know crooks. He said he found out that Hughes and Young are leaders of rival gangs. Sherwin never worked with anybody else, so the investigator couldn't find out much about him. Also, the story among the crooks is that the man who headed up this job has a clean record with the police."

"Beagle, you're terrific!" I said. "I thought we were going to have to go out and talk to the crooks ourselves. Thanks to this new information, I think I know who stole the Lockridge diamonds. Just give me a minute to add your clues to the notes I already have."

Below the names of the suspects, I had the following clues:

1. Lightfingers Ted Young, a member of a gang suspected of shoplifting, is the only one of the suspects who has ever been in prison.
2. The thief is a member of a gang.
3. Sherwin has always worked alone.

4. Hughes and Young are leaders of rival gangs.
5. The thief has never been caught by the police.

	gang member	no prison record
LIGHTFINGERS TED YOUNG		
BUZZ HUGHES		
LOUIS SHERWIN		

[Find the person who is both a gang member and free of any criminal record and you will have identified the thief. Check your solution against Ellen's on the following page.]

Solution to "The Big Diamond Robbery":

Lightfingers Ted Young has been in prison, but the diamond thief does not have a police record, so Lightfingers did not steal the diamonds.

The diamond thief is a member of a gang. Since Louis Sherwin works alone, he is not the diamond thief.

So that means that Buzz Hughes and his gang were responsible for the theft of Mrs. Lockridge's diamonds.

With the field narrowed to one, the police took just two hours to find the evidence they needed to arrest Buzz Hughes.

"You see," Beagle said. "We didn't fail. You found the thief."

"No, Beagle, *we* found the thief. Without the facts you collected, I couldn't have solved the case. But we didn't find the diamonds, and the police haven't either," I added.

"Never mind," Beagle said. "Tomorrow is another day."

■12■

The Missing Diamonds

W hen Beagle didn't show up or call today, I went over to our office to find out if there was any news about Mrs. Lockridge's diamonds.

"The police have rounded up the entire Buzz Hughes gang. I just heard the news on the radio. Let's go talk to Captain Holloway and see what he has found out," Beagle said.

At the police station, the first thing we heard was that all the gang, except for Buzz Hughes himself, had been questioned and released for lack of evidence.

Captain Holloway met us with a big smile of welcome. "Have a seat. I'll tell you what we know so far."

"Have you found out where the diamonds are?" I asked.

"I'm afraid we still don't have them," the captain told us. "We have questioned all four members of the gang. Incidentally, the gang members are Ben Stayman, Max Tolman, Cliff Fairley and Elmo Becker. Buzz, someone who served as the get-away driver, and another man (who is their fence) are probably the only ones we will be able to charge with this theft."

"Fence?" Beagle asked. "You mean something like a sword fighter?"

Captain Holloway smiled. "No, *fence* is a term for a person who sells stolen goods. Under questioning, Buzz has admitted that three people argued about the diamonds. He said they were Ben Stayman, the get-away driver, and the fence. The fence got possession of the jewelry, which he is going to hold until it can be broken apart and the diamonds sold separately. If we only knew which member of the gang acts as their fence, we would know where to look for the stolen jewels.

"When we questioned Elmo Becker, he offered to reveal the identity of the driver, whom he dislikes, in return for leniency for himself and his friend Ben Stayman. Cliff Fairley told the fence not to sell the diamonds until the gang agrees on a division of money. Max Tolman, the driver, and the fence all three own handguns. That's about all we have learned," Captain Holloway concluded.

We thanked Captain Holloway for being willing to include us in the case. "We really appreciate it," I told him.

"Everybody knows you are responsible for the arrest of Buzz Hughes. Maybe you'll help us find the diamonds," the captain said.

Back in our office, I sat down to study the clues. Beagle made a list of the suspects with addresses for each one. When he finished a bag of potato chips, he said he was going to look for something else to eat and set off for the house at a fast trot.

I was drawing the chart below my list of clues when the door of the shed swung open.

"Did you happen to bring an apple with you?" I asked without looking up.

At the next moment a dark cloth was dropped over my head, a hand was clamped over my mouth, and I was lifted roughly from my chair. I couldn't scream, but I did kick.

It didn't do me much good, though, because I was

dumped into the trunk of a car where I bounced around in the dark as the car raced over the streets.

When the car stopped, I was dragged out and blindfolded. Next, I was tied hand and foot, and then I was dropped on a hard cement floor. I heard metallic sounds and guessed that someone was opening a safe. Finally, I heard footsteps and a door slamming as my captor went away. I was suddenly afraid that I was going to lie there forever.

I didn't know where I was or who had kidnapped me, but I could make a good guess that my kidnapper was also the fence. He had come here to pick up the diamonds and make his escape. Tying me up was just a way of giving himself a little extra time to get away. Maybe it would have been better if the police had not been so willing to give me credit for solving the case.

After what seemed like the first half of forever, I heard a door opening and footsteps coming my way.

"Ellen," someone whispered.

It is not easy to recognize a whisper, but I knew that voice. It was Beagle! I made what noises I could. They came out sounding like "Ummm! Errggg!" And then I felt Beagle fumbling with the ropes on my hands.

In seconds I was free of the ropes and blindfold. But I still couldn't see.

"It's pitch-dark in here," I said.

"I know. We're in a warehouse."

"How did you find me?" I asked.

"You left your notebook behind. I used the clues and your chart to learn who had the diamonds. Then I just had to hope the same person had you. I know he owns this warehouse, and I got here as fast as I could. I'm sorry about the delay, but I'm not as fast at those puzzles as you are."

[Would you have been able to find Ellen? Here is the information Beagle found in her notebook:

1. Ben Stayman had fought with the get-away driver and the fence for possession of the diamonds; and the fence had won.

2. Elmo Becker had offered to tell the police who the get-away driver was in return for leniency for himself and his friend Ben Stayman.

3. Cliff Fairley told the fence not to sell the jewels yet.

4. Max Tolman, the driver and the fence all owned handguns.

	Driver	Fence
ELMO BECKER		
MAX TOLMAN		
CLIFF FAIRLEY		
BEN STAYMAN		

Turn the page to check your solution with Beagle's.]

Solution to "The Missing Diamonds":

The first clue eliminates Ben Stayman as the driver and as the fence.

From clue #2, Beagle knew that Elmo Becker was not the driver.

Cliff Fairley is not the fence, clue #3.

Clue #4 means that Max Tolman is neither the driver nor the fence.

Therefore, Becker is the fence, and Cliff Fairley drove the get-away car.

Beagle had just apologized for not getting there sooner when the lights came on.

"Well, well," Beagle said. "You must be Elmo Becker. You're the fence for the Buzz Hughes gang."

"And I thought the girl here was the only one with brains. You're a bright kid, but it's not going to do you any good," Elmo said, pointing a gun at Beagle.

Just once in his whole life Beagle had done something unselfish. Why, I wondered, did it also have to be something stupid?

"Now we're both in trouble," I said.

90

"I guess so," Beagle said. "Pretty dumb of me to come here, huh?"

The really dumb thing was that he was grinning.

And then I saw why.

Captain Holloway stepped through the door behind Elmo Becker.

"Drop it, Becker. This little stunt is going to put you in jail for a long time," Captain Holloway said.

Later, as Becker was being led away in handcuffs, Holloway explained that Becker had moved the jewels from the warehouse safe to his car, where the police found them, all still in their original settings.

"How did you manage to find us?" I asked Captain Holloway.

"Your friend here called us as soon as he figured out who had the diamonds just before he set off to find you himself."

"I'm glad you got here when you did. I was counting on you," Beagle said. "I don't think we had a minute to spare."

"Mrs. Lockridge is going to be very grateful to you," Captain Holloway said, "and I'm grateful, too. Can we count on your help again?"

I was about to say "sure." But Beagle spoke first.

"Not for a while," he said. "This detecting can get pretty scary. The Beagle Detective Agency is closing for a vacation."

By the last light of the setting sun, I watched Beagle nail a new sign to the door of his shed.

CLOSED UNTIL SEPTEMBER

"That's it for mysteries," Beagle said. "It's time to take a break from detecting."

How could Beagle be so cheerful? I personally felt pretty glum at the prospect of the rest of the summer without mysteries. "So what are you going to do, Beagle?" I asked.

"Oh, I've got a really good friend who is going to spend the rest of the month fishing with me," he answered promptly.

No wonder he didn't mind closing up the agency. Obviously his plans were already made. The funny thing was that I had never thought of Beagle as having any friends, much less a really good one.

"So who is it you're going fishing with?" I asked.

"You know, Ellen, for one super-smart detective,

you are sometimes very slow to figure things out," Beagle said.

"What do you mean?"

"I mean I'll see you tomorrow. I'll bring the worms. You bring the sandwiches."